Little Red Riding Hood

Manufactured in the U.S.A.

8   7   6   5   4   3   2   1

ISBN 1-56173-916-2

Cover illustration by Sam Thiewes

Book illustrations by Susan Spellman

Story adapted by Jane Jerrard

Publications International, Ltd.

long time ago, there was a tiny village near a large forest. At the very end of the village, on the edge of the forest, lived a little girl and her mother.

The girl's grandmother, who loved her more than kittens love mischief, had made her granddaughter a beautiful red velvet riding cloak with a hood. The girl wore the hooded cloak all the time. She wore it so much that the other villagers called her Little Red Riding Hood.

One day, Little Red Riding Hood's mother asked her to take a big basket of food to her kindly grandmother, who was feeling sick.

"Go quickly, dear, and don't wander around in the forest. Stay on the path. Grandmother is waiting," she told her little daughter. Little Red Riding Hood promised to go straight to her grandmother's. She put on her red cloak and set out right away.

Now her grandmother's house was deep inside the forest. But Little Red Riding Hood knew which path to take, and was not a bit afraid to walk by herself. She was not even afraid when she met a big wolf that day!

"Good morning," said the wolf.

"Good morning, Mr. Wolf," said Little Red Riding Hood.

Now the wolf, as you probably know, was a wicked animal, and not to be trusted. But he was very polite when he spoke to Little Red Riding Hood.

"Where are you going, little girl?" the wolf asked.

"To Grandmother's house," she said. "I am taking this basket of food to her because she is sick." She happily answered all his questions. She even told him where her grandmother lived and how to get there!

While she chatted, that wicked wolf was thinking about how much he'd like to eat Little Red Riding Hood and her basket of food.

As the wolf walked with Little Red Riding Hood, he said, "You are marching along as if you were on your way to school! You should play awhile and pick some flowers!"

Little Red Riding Hood looked around her. Seeing what a pretty day it was, she thought the wolf was right. She *should* enjoy the morning and pick some wildflowers for her grandmother.

So she left the path and started to gather the prettiest flowers she could find. She daydreamed a little as she searched—and she forgot all about her promise to her mother.

Meanwhile, the wolf crept down the path until he was out of sight. Then he ran straight to Grandmother's house, lickety-split. Once he'd caught his breath, he knocked gently on the door.

"Who is it?" called Grandmother.

"It is Little Red Riding Hood. I've brought you some cake and bread and butter," said the wicked wolf.

"Lift the latch and come in," said Grandmother, for she was tucked in bed. But when she saw the wolf step in, she leaped right up, only to faint from fright!

The wolf, wanting only to eat tender Little Red Riding Hood, rolled the poor old woman under the bed. Then he disguised himself with her lacy cap and nightgown and jumped into her bed. And there he waited.

When Little Red Riding Hood had picked an armload of perfect little wildflowers, she remembered her sick grandmother and her promise to her mother. She rushed to her grandmother's house, and knocked on the door.

"Who is it?" called the wolf, sounding just like Little Red Riding Hood's grandmother.

"It is I, Little Red Riding Hood," called the girl.

"Lift the latch and come in," said the wolf.

Little Red Riding Hood *thought* she saw her grandmother lying in bed, with her lacy cap pulled low and the covers pulled up to her chin.

The wolf said, "Come closer, my dear," in a high, quavering voice. Little Red Riding Hood came right up to the bedside.

"My, Grandmother, what big ears you have!" she said, taking a step back.

"The better to hear you with, my dear," said the wolf.

"What big eyes you have, Grandmother!" said Little Red Riding Hood, taking another step back.

"The better to see you with, my dear."

"But, Grandmother, what big teeth you have!"

"The better to EAT you with!" cried the wolf.

And with that, the wolf leaped out of the bed and chased Little Red Riding Hood around the room! He was very hungry and had been looking forward to eating the little girl. But Little Red Riding Hood was too quick for the big bad wolf. She jumped out of his reach and ran to the door.

Luckily for Little Red Riding Hood, the wolf was not used to wearing Grandmother's nightgown. He kept stumbling and tripping over the hem and had a hard time chasing Little Red Riding Hood.

Little Red Riding Hood ran straight out the open door. "Help! Help! A wolf!" she cried.

It happened that a hunter, who had been after that wicked wolf for days, was in the woods nearby. He had followed the wolf's footprints right up to the path to Grandmother's house.

When the hunter heard Little Red Riding Hood's cries for help, the hunter raised his gun as quick as a wink and shot the wolf dead as he leaped through the door of Grandmother's house.

Little Red Riding Hood and the hunter went inside to find poor Grandmother rising to her feet, covered with dust from head to toe. Little Red Riding Hood ran to her arms.

hen she heard about their narrow escape from the wicked wolf, Grandmother insisted on a party to thank the kind hunter. So Little Red Riding Hood, the hunter, and Grandmother sat down at the kitchen table and shared the basket of good things to eat.

And forever after, Little Red Riding Hood always obeyed her mother and never left the path when she walked in the woods.